Theft on the Generation Ship

Science Fiction Short Story

Newsletter

Sign Up to my Newsletter.

- Learn first about new Releases.

- Read exclusive background information.

- Get special fan extras.

Sign up here:

Or here:
https://blog.topazhauyn.com/newsletter/

for me

Theft on the Generation Ship

Science Fiction Short Story

Topaz Hauyn

Visit us online:
www.topazhauyn.com

ISBN: 9798794996692
Font: Alegreya
Coverdesign: Topaz Hauyn
Art: Golden Sikorka/depositphotos.com

Marlene Goodyear read the report in front of her.

Her thoughts veered sideways mid-list.

She thought about her wardrobe with the little options she had. Should she wear the red dress again? It fit perfect to her red hair and tan skin.

Or should she choose the white one leaving her shoulders bare, to symbolize her hope for Ricks save return?

Her back hurt from the hard aluminum chair she sat on but more from the days work.

Marlene sat in her small office. She aimed to finish the yearly inventory for the drug store, that was in front of her office. As shopkeeper, it was her duty to finish them on time.

Marlene's eyelids felt heavy. She was tired.

The day with all the counting for inventories sake had been long. Even with Benny helping her and the shop closed today.

Her legs felt sore from all the kneeling, bending over and standing on tiptoe to reach all racks.

She wanted to return to her private two-room apartment with her soft bed. Only the outlook at her weekly, virtual date with Rick Weiss, her boyfriend, and soon-to-be husband tonight kept her going.

She would, thankful for having some extra shower heads at shoulder and hip height, take a shower first thing coming home.

Rick deserved to see her as relaxed and positive as possible on their weekly video date.

In front of Marlene's chair hovered a semitransparent projection, the screen, of the inventory list created today. She had to go through the list.

A dull duty. She did this job for ten years now. Never had been anything wrong with the inventory.

The time in the lower right of the screen told Marlene she had one hour left until her scheduled meeting with Rick. Somehow she had to manage to dress herself up. Rick preferred to see her dressed up.

Marlene could understand his wish. And with the prospect of rarely seeing her husband-to-be, she was willing to fulfill his wish once a week. She preferred comfortable clothes, like huge shirts and comfy sports pants at home.

Rick was on duty at one of the outposts. His job was to make sure none of the many asteroids, dust and other, human based trash, hit their space city.

Usually he slept in one of the quarters at the outpost.

With four hours to travel to the quarter of the city, where she lived and led the drug store, she would do the same.

Marlene looked forward to Rick's next month off duty. It was another three months away. Then they would marry and work on their own children.

The white dress then, decided Marlene.

Hope was always a good thing to show.

After all, it was all they had in their space city. The hope of not being hit by an asteroid. The hope of finding a new inhabitable planet one day.

Marlene remembered some stories from her grandparents about Earth. She knew the old pictures of the blue planet and the marvelous protection moon gave Earth. But the little planet circling around the Earth couldn't prevent it from human destruction.

To Marlene all those stories and pictures felt like any other tale she heard as a child. She knew nothing else than this city. And she would never learn anything else. The scientists calculated with four or five more generations before reaching an inhabitable planet.

Sad thing, none of the scientists had yet managed to create a moon for their flying city. The news had it, that they had enough to do to keep the city running.

At some lone nights or dull tasks, doubts about the sense of her life crept at Marlene. Like now, doing the inventory. There was no money around, just some shops to fake an economy she only knew from textbooks.

Marlene took in another breath of the metallic air. It was thick and stalled. Maybe tomorrow, when her weekend started she would have a chance to visit one of the gardens to breathe some fresh air. She would have to check the waiting list.

Marlene tapped her index finger on the projection to scroll down the inventory list. Benny, her new shop assistant, did half of the work today.

She was very glad for having Benny.

He was silent, lean and could think on his own. The contrary of his predecessor, Xaver, who was thick and therefore always, accidentally, knocked against things on the shelves. Many things dropped. Lots of shards of glass to clean up. Many long hours to clean up leading to missed dates with Rick.

Shuddering Marlene thought at the heated discussions she had to go through. Each time she missed one of the weekly dates Rick implied she didn't value their relationship enough. She hated his shouting.

Marlene looked around her little office.

The gray door opposite of her hard aluminum chair, led to the showroom. Left of her was a keyboard she could pull over to type in things manually. Above it were some cupboards with product samples to look at. She still had to decide the order in which she wanted to add them to her shops' product range.

The clock on the screen said she had daydreamed for a good ten minutes.

Marlene pulled herself together to scan through the inventory list. Thankfully the computer calculated numbers of what should be in the store were displayed next to the list with the counted numbers.

She scrolled through it faster, searching for any red lines, indicating number differences.

Her stomach rumbled. She had skipped lunch to speed things up. No need to get another discussion with Rick.

Four red lines appeared. They stopped Marlene cold.

She stared at the lines. This couldn't be. This had to be an error in the display.

She pressed recalculate.

Nothing changed. The lines stayed red.

Ten packages of silk stockings, one pregnancy test, two bottles of maple molasses and three packages of condoms lacked.

Marlene sat up straight.

The chair followed her movement, provided the hard backrest to her new position. The screen adjusted too, to perfect distance and height relative to her face.

She wiped over her forehead with the sleeve of her blue shirt. It got wet from her sweat. She felt cold, fearing more missing things.

Marlene scrolled through the remaining list. Everything else was fine.

Relieved at that she leaned back a bit.

What could she do with this?

The textbooks she memorized years back said, she had to call the security team and file a complaint.

But why would anybody steal those things from her drug store on the first hand? Everyone got everything one needed. No need for theft.

And, more important, how did he accomplish this with everything secured electronically?

The tie to the security system could only be released on payment at the self-service checkout. With payment meaning, identifying, so the system knew to whom the resources were given.

Nothing more.

Money had been abandoned long ago. Everyone had a task in the city, fitting his ability and liking. Aside from that, their main duty was to give birth to children that could one day reach a new home planet.

Marlene touched the pocket of her loose pair of trousers. The hard, inflexible, rectangular ID card was in it. This was the second way to release the tie to the security system, thanks to her authority as the shopkeeper.

She only used it to remove the broken items from the system.

She scratched her head. Never before did she experience a theft. Their city might be large with about a thousand inhabitants, yet, nobody could leave it.

At least not alive.

Marlene touched a few points on her screen, sent the inventory lists to the background. With the video communication in the front, she connected to the security team.

"Good evening. I'd like to report a theft in the drug store on the Main Street 49", said Marlene.

"Good evening, Mrs. Goodyear. I am Robin Land", said a man with short brown hair and blue eyes on her screen. "I see your theft items. Yet, there is no way our system can be tricked."

Marlene smiled at the man. "Mr. Land, I know this. Yet, those items are missing."

"Did you check under the shelves? Maybe they are in the wrong place?", asked Mr. Land.

Marlene knew he was trying to help her. But her shelf had no space at the bottom where anything could roll under. Neither were their holes at the back.

"Negative, Mr. Land. I'm doing inventory for ten years now. Never had been anything lost", said Marlene. "There has to be a way around the system. And I've already checked. My ID card is with me."

Mr. Land smiled on her screen.

To Marlene, he didn't look like he believed her.

She had the hunch she had to find out herself what happened. If she wanted to prove there was any way around the security system.

"Why don't you come and check yourself?", asked Marlene.

Mr. Land shook his head.

"I am sorry, on site research isn't included in our task description. Otherwise, we would do an inventory any day at another store. Go count yourself again first, please."

He closed the connection.

Marlene stared at the screen. She couldn't believe the security team rejected her try to file a complaint.

She bit her lower lip.

Her time ran out. Only half an hour left until her date with Rick.

It felt wrong to her to leave her business without solving this.

Marlene got up. Her chair moved sideways to the keyboard on the wall, making space for her to walk up and down the narrow room.

Four steps forward, turn. Her shoes scratched over the gray floor. Four steps forward, turn again.

Marlene went to check the stockings. Fourteen packages should be in the store. Four were still there. Ten missing, like the numbers on the screen said.

She had no clue whom she was looking for, but why not try it with one of the tricks that worked in the ancient tales?

She pulled the daily videos from her store of the last week.

"Check for customers looking like me, or customers with huge bags", said Marlene to her computer.

Within minutes, she got three clients. A red-haired woman she identified as her younger sister, Anita. A red-haired woman with a fat figure. The computer called her Mrs. Claw and listed her as suspicious. A boy, maybe sixteen years, with one of those ugly, black, shapeless backpacks used to store snacks.

Marlene called Mrs. Claw via video connection. Usually she didn't use the information she could get on her customers, but she wanted to check the suspects she got.

The fat, hanging cheeks of the red-haired woman flashed on Marlene's screen. Connection established, said the message below.

Marlene saw some white packages in the background of Mrs. Claw. She couldn't read the names on them. But the size could fit the silk stockings.

"Good evening, Mrs. Claw", said Marlene. "I am sorry to interrupt your evening. I am Mrs. Goodyear, the shopkeeper of the drug store in Main Street 49. Did you buy silk stockings in my shop last week?"

"Good evening, Mrs. Goodyear. You should know better. It's your shop", said Mrs. Claw.

Marlene felt her stomach tie into a knot. She could have. But not if the woman found a way around check out.

Mrs. Claw sounded annoyed from the call, maybe a bit angry. She rose her voice. "Why do you call me to ask?"

Marlene made sure her smile stayed on her face. A professional smile. With her voice completely free of emotions, strictly businesslike she answered: "We had an issue with our system and need to solve some glitches."

"I bought no silk stockings at your store", said Mrs. Claw. "Why would I? The ones from my family stash are way better."

Mrs. Claw held up a rectangular, white vintage package, with a female lower body, clad in stockings.

Marlene forced her shock back. What a rude presentation of legs in public. Her actual packages where white cubes with the name of the product printed on top. No art, no pictures.

"I see. Thank you", said Marlene.

She closed the connection. Too surprised by the alien packaging to think of any more questions.

Marlene whipped of the sweat from her forehead.

Her office had turned way too hot in the last minute.

Better she left this mess for Monday. If the security team wanted her to recount everything, she surely wouldn't do it now. Her bed was waiting for her sore legs and aching shoulders.

Before Marlene reached the door, her screen showed an incoming call from Anita., her little sister.

"Hi, sis. I need your help", said Anita.

As always without any small talk or even the word please in her sentences.

Marlene rolled her eyes.

She sighted, pulled out her chair from her left and sat down.

"Hello to you too, Anita. I am glad you are fine and healthy", said Marlene. "What's the problem this time?"

She crossed her fingers hoping she could solve it quickly to return to her main problem. Or finally go home.

Her sister surely had nothing to do with it. She had even helped her last week at Xaver's last day to clean the remaining shards of glass. She even worked a day at the shop until Benny came to take over the assistants duties.

Marlene saw her time melting like an ice asteroid approaching a sun.

She wouldn't have time for her massage showers any more now. She had to even do a rush on the makeup to be on time.

But Anita had helped her before, she couldn't let her down without listening.

"My homework assignment isn't done", said Anita brushing her red curls behind her ear with the glittering sun shaped earring. "The teacher wants it at the full hour. I still need some history details. Tell me whatever you know about Earth."

"About Earth?", asked Marlene. "I know as much as you do. Look up the old files."

"Something private. Family stories and the such. Not the official stuff", said Anita. "You're older. You knew grandma and grandpa better!"

Marlene thought back. Sure. No big deal. She was eleven older than Anita.

She stretched her neck and rolled her hurting shoulders feeling her ponytail pulling her head backwards with its weight. The thin fabric of her blue shirt stretched from the movement. The wet spot on her sleeve send a cold shiver over her arm. A stark contrast to the hot room around her.

"Tell you what. Back on Earth they had pictures from women wearing silk stocking on their packages", said Marlene.

"You made that up", said Anita. Arms crossed, tips of her mouth pulled down.

"No. I saw such a package a minute before", said Marlene. "A customer showed me one from her families stash. Meanwhile: What did you buy at my store last week?"

"A box of fruit tea. Mine was empty", said Anita.

"No stockings, or condoms, or maple molasses, or pregnancy test?", asked Marlene, going through her list of stolen items.

"NO!", shouted Anita. "What the hell do you think from me? I don't need a pregnancy test!"

The rage of her sister seemed true to Marlene.

Anita was rude at times, yet she did respect the rules which matched the couples to avoid children with dense degrees of kinship.

"Okay. I helped you. Anything else?", asked Marlene. "I'd like to go home. Forget this stupid day and call Rick, like every Friday evening."

Marlene saw Anita opening her mouth.

Marlene pressed her crossed fingers tighter together. Her time passed by too quick. Please let her have nothing else. She needed some time to reach her two-room apartment, too.

"Thank you. Tell Rick I said hello", said Anita.

Miriam smashed the office door shut behind her, locked the drug store door and ran home as fast as possible.

Marlene shut her gray apartment door behind her.

She leaned against the metal door for a moment to catch her breath.

She stood at the entrance of her living room.

The air in her living room was slightly better than at her office and outside on the gangways. The concealed smell lingered everywhere. She could only escape it in the gardens where the gardeners grew food, and partly at home.

She inhaled deeply the light scent of fresh air coming from living plants. Thanks to the group of five green pot plants standing on the circular table in front of her.

Besides the fresh air, the plants added color to her live. All the gray doors, walls, ceilings. She hated them.

She kicked her flat shoes aside and stepped on the fluffy purple carpet on the floor. Another one of her changes in trying to add color to her life.

At least at home.

With closed eyes she took in the feeling of soft surface, caressing her naked feet. She wiggled her toes.

The clock at the wall next to her said she had one minute left.

Marlene let out her breath.

She stroked the loose strands of her red hair back behind her ears. She sat down on the curved, comfortable chair next to her desk and leaned back.

This one was way better than the one in her back office. It was made from aluminum too, but designed to be a place to relax. Not a place to sit ergonomically and work for hours.

“Screen turn on. Connect to Rick Weiss”, said Marlene.

She tried to breathe more regular. She was still breathless from her sprint home.

Next to her appeared a semitransparent holograph. The screen displayed a circle spinning. Connection was on its way.

Marlene took in another deep breath.

Sweat poured out all over her body. She felt soaked in it. Sad thing she couldn’t make it earlier to take a shower. Gloomy she stared at the door opposite the entrance door. Behind it was her bedroom. There waited her white dress. Dry-cleaned, ironed, hanging in the drawer.

Tomorrow, she promised to herself, for the fourth time this month, she would start again at regular gymnastics.

Her shirt was too tight. Her condition was down.

She needed to practice more.

Waiting for the computer to set up the connection, Marlene looked at her potted plants.

They were all of different kinds, although she forgot their names long ago.

One had small, long, green leaves with a white stripe in the middle. She touched the soft surface of the long leave with her finger. It felt dry. They probably needed water like she did after her sprint.

Another plant was shaped like a little ball with thorns all around. The other three had some oval leaves.

Marlene remembered the plants in the gardens to flower once a year. She couldn't remember hers ever having flowers. Maybe she should consult one of the gardeners about this.

Marlene's breath calmed down.

She looked at the semitransparent screen hovering at the side of her desk. It still showed a circle spinning. The clock said her, two minutes already passed.

Marlene felt stupid for rushing home.

Rick obviously wasn't home yet.

She got up, turned and walked through the third door to the kitchen. She fetched a bottle of water from the white deposition next to the silvery kitchen sink.

But why was Rick not home? Was there a problem at the outpost? Was he injured?

Never ever had Rick been late before.

It was her job to be late now and then. And he always made sure to let her know how lazy he thought her for those delays.

Another minute passed.

Marlene drank from her bottle. The water was warm as always.

She watered the pot plants. Put the bottle down on the gray table next to the pots.

Her thoughts wandered back to the stolen items in her drug store.

She couldn't wrap her head around the fact, anybody got to lengths to trick the system.

Marlene walked around her round table. She couldn't calm her thoughts.

She switched her screen to the news.

Nothing.

Waiting for Rick to answer her call, Marlene opened her inventory files on the screen. Something nagged at her. Something she missed.

She checked the list of items removed as broken by her. There were perfume bottles and glasses. But not one of the four missing items.

Marlene opened the archived calls with Mrs. Claw and Anita.

She had a hunch something was off. She had overseen a detail.

Searching for it, she listened to both conversations again.

There. In the call with Anita, she found it.

Anita, wasn't at home. The background wasn't the usual gray from all around the city. There was a little painting on the wall. A green leave from her pot plant with the long, small, light green leaves.

Marlene still remembered the day she met Rick for the first time. It was the matching day, held once a year.

The computer sent her into the room where Rick already leaned against the gray wall. His dark blue jacket, trousers and boots from work still on. His name tag clear on his chest.

He had smiled at her, when she entered.

Marlene remembered how fascinated she had been by the touch of his hand. The stroke of his fingers over her arms.

His black eyes had looked friendly. Until she gifted him her little painting.

Stupid leisure activity, had he called it. But he took it with him. Each time she called it on duty, she saw it on the wall.

What had Anita done at Rick's place?

Marlene wondered.

She had a bad feeling.

Anita never visited the outposts before. Neither did she.

She checked the call to Rick.

Pending.

"Abort connection. Call Ricks supervisor", said Marlene.

Her own voice sounded thin to her.

Anita had only denied the need for condoms. Had she had a use for the other items?

"Hello, Mrs. Goodyear", said Ricks supervisor, an older man with a brown beard, on the screen. "What's the matter?"

"Hello. I can't get my weekly connection call to Mr. Weiss. Is he still on duty?", asked Marlene.

The man looked upwards for a moment.

She could feel him searching for patience.

Marlene felt stupid for calling him.

"Surely you have important work to do", said Marlene. "I'm sorry I've interrupted you. I'll try it later again."

She stretched her finger to end the call.

"It's alright. He went home an hour ago", said the man slowly.

Marlene watched him check something on another screen she couldn't see.

"I'll call you back in a minute. Don't leave your apartment", said the supervisor in a firm voice.

What?

Marlene stared at him. Or better. She stared at the empty screen.

Did this man really give her an order?

Her worries build. Something was wrong.

Terribly wrong.

She felt it in the bad gut feeling. Her throat felt tight.

She waited.

The screen in front of her showed nothing but the purple carpet and the gray edge of her round table shimmering through it.

Her mouth felt dry.

She took another gulp from the gray bottle she placed on the table.

With a little rustle she put it back there.

Her formerly comfortable chair, become hard and unfitting.

What had Anita done at Rick's place when she called her earlier?

The screen changed, opened a video connection.

First thing Marlene saw was her hand drawn picture on the wall.

It was smeared with something brown.

She felt the pain of Ricks condemnation coming back. But why had he ruined the picture now? One year after she gave it to him?

Marlene looked at the supervisor standing in front of her.

He wore the navy blue jacket and trousers Rick wore at the outpost too. His face had turned from friendly searching for patience to hard and determined.

"Mrs. Goodyear, when did you talk to Mr. Weiss the last time?", asked the supervisor.

"Last week", said Marlene.

What kind of question was this?

"What happened?", asked Marlene.

"Mr. Weiss is dead", said the supervisor. He held his hands firm behind his head.

Marlene gasped for air. This was a bad joke. It couldn't be.

How should Rick die in his quarter?

"Negative. The log files say you talked to him about fifteen minutes ago", said the supervisor. "In person."

"No! I've been in my office trying to solve a burglary", said Marlene.

Why would the log files say something different? Despair filled her. Truth to be told. She hadn't liked Rick that much. But she had looked forward to their wedding. Looked forward to having children on her own. If Rick was dead she would never have children.

Would she be allowed to stay alive? Without giving birth, her meaning of life on the space city was over.

"What happened to Rick?", asked Marlene.

The picture changed.

There was a net of thin light brown lines woven over the floor. In front of it was a lot of light brown liquid that seemed to stick to Rick's booth that still laid there. A motionless leg.

She couldn't see more of him.

"Silk stockings and maple molasses?" Marlene choked the words out of her mouth.

"Right", said the supervisors cold voice. "And frozen water used as a weapon it seems."

"I haven't been at his quarter", said Marlene.

Panic rose in her chest. She needed to get out of her apartment. She needed fresh air.

This had been Anita's work. But why? And how?

The questions bounced inside her head.

Marlene stood.

She shook. The room was shaking too.

"Mrs. Goodyear. Sit down!", commanded the supervisor. "When you weren't here. Who else looks like you?"

"My sister", whispered Marlene. "Anita. She looks similar. She was there. I called her and didn't realize it she was there."

Marlene watched the gray, little cube laying in her hand.

It felt light and cold. Cold like she felt since that awful Friday evening a week ago.

With Rick's murder she became a widow before becoming a wife.

The cube didn't fill her palm. Inside was the ash of Rick. Everything that remained from him.

Marlene was alone in the wide, white hall at the center of the space city.

The low vibration from the engine below her felt like she was little again. Little and being rocked in her mothers arms.

The wall in front of her was filled with small shelf's. Each large enough for one cube to add.

Marlene blinked. Her tears rolled from her eyes down her cheeks. Now she could read the letters on the cube.

"Rick Weiss, 34 years, 3rd generation."

With her archived phone call, Ricks supervisor had enough proof to match the log files with Anita's presence. Even the amount of silk stockings, spilled maple molasses and ice filled condoms matched the missing number of packages from Marlene's drug store.

Marlene carefully placed Rick's cube in one of the empty spots.

She would live. Like Anita who was pregnant. Of course, she didn't need the condoms anymore. Not for their intended purpose anyway.

Marlene turned around, ready to continue her life.

The computer had already assigned her another man.

The security team was still searching for the error in their system.

Marlene didn't care anymore. She already applied for working at the gardeners team.

THE END

Excerpt:
The Water Theft

Gravity was reinstalled on the ship. They had safely left Sowa and were now heading home.

Zelon looked down at the screens in front of him. Everything was alright. The water was safely stored in the tanks. They could leave Sowa now, flying back to their home planet. The route was calculated and the speed was adjusted to the extra weight and inertia added by their valuable cargo. The energy would be more than enough to bring them home to Xarthe. Zelon stretched his arms and moved his shoulders in circles to eliminate the tension from the travel so far. He felt much more relaxed now and his staff members slowly started to relax too.

He turned to the water dispenser and filled a glass for himself. The water looked like it always did. Crystal clear. He took the first sip. There was no taste on his tongue. It was clean and fresh water. No comparison to the rehashed water he drunk on his way to Sowa. The rehashed water always had a bitter taste and was somehow stale. Yet it fulfilled it's purpose, keeping them alive.

He finished his glass and looked around. Everyone waited for him to give the command.

"Let's go", Zelon said and the crew on the bridge started the engines for the long distance jump, which would bring them close to home. Soon Sowa was a little point on their star map, and they were on their way.

Zelon walked around the bridge inspecting the different terminals, his officers were monitoring, navigating or working on. A task he would have preferred to do from his place. But he couldn't read the reports on the captains console. Security reasons, had his father said, when Zelon had complained for the first time. His console was in its own network on the ship. Connected to the weapon system. Weapons he shouldn't have, given his spaceship was a transporter and an old one, although it was very reliable. He made do with the extra work despite the itching, too tight clothes that were full of mud from the water gathering.

Everyone one of his officers he passed signaled okay
with a snap of their finger: Fuel, health environment
on the ship, other observations, communications, and
clear space ahead for the flight home. They could make
the jump alright.

Back on his place, Zelon waited and observed the
jump. Only a few more hours to fly home through space.
Time for a little pause, he decided. This would give him
the chance to change clothes and get rid of the mud
and dust he was covered in from being on Sowa. He
logged out of the captains console, waved his first officer
Maurke on his place and turned to the door. A bit of
reading and a refreshing syrup bread would be great
after changing into comfortable Xarthian clothes. They
had much more room to move, instead of those tight
and stiff Sowan trousers and shirts.

Excerpt end of: The Water Theft

More books

Fantasy

Beaten Path in the Mist
Vampire Hunting with the Tiger Eye
Marlene's New Monster
Remorse of the Mermaid
Wipe off the Dust
The Book Burning
Stars Flying into Philosophy
Red: #890000
The True Mage Survives
The Flower on the Mountain Top
The speaking Mirror

The Fork with the Scales
Fairy Needs Courage
The Rainbow Bubble Collapse
Repair the Music
The missing Jack O'Lantern

Wishing Well World
- A Fairies Wish (#1)
- Fantasy Sweets (#2)
- Hodur at Christmas Eve (#3)

Merchant Universe
- Merchant of all Power (#1)
- Lifa's first trade (#2)

Romance

M/F, Hetero Romantik
World Cup and Pink Ropes
An Invitation to a Wedding
Corrupted Food Storage
Fighting the Cinnamon Guy
Forgotten Communications
The Magic Book
Love against all Rules
Love as a Christmas Present
The Griffin's Wedding Ring
Crossroads with Half the

Information (Collection)
Love over Tomato Soup

Secret Southwest Forest Shifters
- Welcome my Wolf (#1)
- Research my Wolf (#2)
- Love my Wolf (#3)
F/F, Lesbische Romantik
Dance to your Love
Reverse Harem / Ménage
Love the Forbidden Partners

Science Fiction

Abandonned Time Travel
Alien Visit
Coloring an Apple

Corrupted Food Storage
Red: #890000
Served like red Wine

Shards of her Life
Support Refused
Sweet Depths
The Water Theft
Lottery Win: The Third Set of
Doors
Human Interactions Preferred

Intertwined Fate
Theft on the Generation Ship
Flying Worlds
- Dicovery (#1)
- Horn of Life (#2)
- Tika discovers the ocean (#3)

Mystery

Eating Out Adventure
Life Changing Game
The Lady Says: Die
The One Time Chance
Intertwined Fate

If date equals…
Keyring
Who paid for the bullet?
Theft on the Generation Ship

Contemporary

The Curses of Operating
Systems
Firefighter Dressed Wrong
Habits burning in the Solar
Eclipse
Wild Majoram

The Rags of an Orphan
Architecture Impress
An Authors first Success
Postcard from a warmer Place
The Meeting Contact
Company Sold

www.ingramcontent.com/pod-product-compliance
Lightning Source LLC
Chambersburg PA
CBHW020852160726
47993CB00004B/1615